A Note for Teachers, Parents and Other Adults

These are the things whose fruits we eat in this world but whose full reward awaits us in the World to Come:

Honoring parents, acts of kindness, arriving early at the house of study morning and evening, hospitality to strangers, visiting the sick, helping the needy bride … devotion to prayer, and bringing peace between people—but the study of Torah is equal to them all.

—from the Babylonian Talmud, Tractate Shabbat 127a

It's a … It's a … It's a Mitzvah is inspired by this Talmud teaching and aims to focus young kids on a contemporary introduction to these good deeds and to God's commandments—*mitzvot.* By highlighting the age-appropriate good deeds mentioned in the Talmud verse and others, it broadens the use of the word *mitzvah* beyond "sacred commandment" to reflect the way most people use it today to include *g'milut hasidim*—acts of lovingkindness. *Mitzvot* include many acts of kindness but they also include other, equally important, holy deeds like learning from the Torah, attending a seder, and resting and playing on Shabbat.

This lively book is filled with likeable animal characters who, through their actions, perform good deeds and acts of lovingkindness of all types. Through playful vignettes, children engage with Jewish wisdom and how the sages instruct us to behave toward each other. For each good deed, the Mitzvah Meerkat congratulates and celebrates the animals' actions with the following exclamation, "It's a … it's a … it's a mitzvah!" The fun-sounding refrain is repeated to encourage children to join in with the reader. We explain each good deed in a sidebar. This gives you an opportunity to ask the child or group of children, "What is the good deed here?" and spark a conversation. Hopefully, the children will guess the act of kindness before you even read the sidebar.

We hope as children become familiar with this book, they will be inspired to become *menschen*—kind souls who think about and help others.

Enjoy!

— Liz Suneby and Diane Heiman

It's a... It's a... It's a

MITZVah

For everyone who has ever touched
my life with acts of kindness, big or small. —LS

For Bruce, Allie, and Carolyn, because of you
I know that love is boundless. —DH

Grateful acknowledgment is given to Stuart M. Matlins, publisher of Jewish Lights, and
Emily Wichland, vice president of Editorial and Production, for having faith in our ideas
and enabling us to share them, and to Laurel Molk for giving spirit to our words.

It's a... It's a... It's a MITZVah

Liz Suneby and Diane Heiman
Illustrations by Laurel Molk

JEWISH LIGHTS Publishing

Woodstock, Vermont

www.jewishlights.com

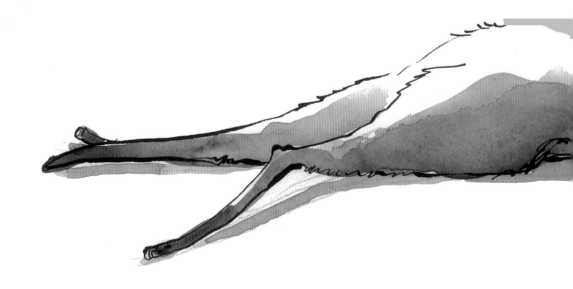

"What's a mitzvah?"

"What's a mitzvah?"

"What's a mitzvah?"

It's a ... it's a ...
it's a mitzvah!

It's a mitzvah to share food with someone who is hungry.

I'm hungry as a bear.

Here, take one sandwich ...

or two, or three, or four,
or five, or six, or
seven …

Whew, I'm getting tired. I guess I'm not a young buck anymore!

It's a ... it's a ... it's a mitzvah!

It's a mitzvah to help someone who is older.

Grandpa, would you like
to rest under that tree?
I'll wait with you.

It's a ... it's a ... it's a mitzvah!

It's a mitzvah to forgive someone for making a mistake.

Whoops—one stick too many! I broke our cozy new lodge.

No worries.
We will rebuild it.

Let's recycle the plastic bottles.

Good thinking, Joey! Please hop on over to the recycle bin for me.

It's a ... it's a ... it's a mitzvah!

It's a mitzvah to take care of the Earth.

It's a ... it's a ...
it's a mitzvah!

It's a mitzvah
to return
something
someone
has lost.

Peter, I found
your mitten!

Thank you.
Has anyone seen
my glasses?

It's a ... it's a ...
it's a mitzvah!

You are such a
good swimmer,
and I barely made
it across the
shallow end.

It's a mitzvah
to cheer on
your friends.

You're doing really well;
you'll be a great
swimmer soon.
I only wish I could run
half as fast as you.

It's a ... it's a ... it's a mitzvah!

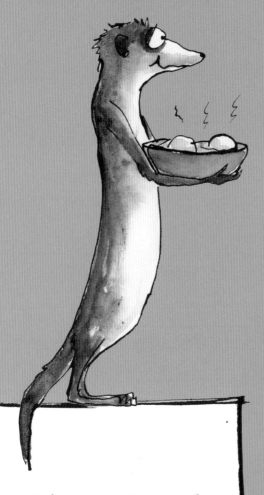

It's a mitzvah to take care of someone who is sick.

Mr. Katz, we heard Lizzy is sick. Here's some homemade chicken soup with oodles of noodles to make her feel better.

Thank you.
Lizzy will love it.

It's a ... it's a ... it's a mitzvah!

It's so nice to knit for those in need.

It's a mitzvah to give *tzedakah* (charity).

Hurry up. You're taking way too long.

There's no need to start a fight.
Give Zoe one more minute.
You can have my turn.

It's a ... it's a ...
it's a mitzvah!

It's a mitzvah
to help make
peace.

Hey, Ellie, it's Friday.
What should we do tonight?

Come to my
house and
share the
loving spirit
of Shabbat.

It's a ... it's a ...
it's a mitzvah!

It's a mitzvah to
enjoy Shabbat
with family and
friends.

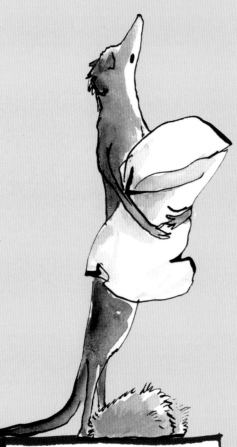

It's a ... it's a ... it's a mitzvah!

It's a mitzvah to honor your parents.

I love it when you read us bedtime stories and sing us bedtime songs.

I love it when you give us bedtime snuggles.

And I love you
all the time!

We know what a mitzvah is.

We know you can't touch it.

We know you can't smell it
(unless it's homemade
chicken soup).

We know you can't buy it.

We know a mitzvah by the warm feeling of happiness in our hearts when we do good deeds.

Mitzvah is a way of life.

That's a ... that's a ... that's a mitzvah!

It's a … It's a … It's a Mitzvah

2012 Hardcover Edition, First Printing
© 2012 by Liz Suneby and Diane Heiman
Illustrations © 2012 by Laurel Molk

Library of Congress Cataloging-in-Publication Data
Heiman, Diane.
It's a— it's a— it's a mitzvah / Diane Heiman and Liz Suneby ; Illustrations by Laurel Molk.
p. cm.
Summary: This lively picture book for children ages 3-6 is filled with amiable animals, who through their actions demonstrate age-appropriate mitzvot, including welcoming new friends, forgiving mistakes, respecting elders, and sharing food with the hungry. It engages children through playful illustrations; likeable animal characters, including Mitzvah Meerkat, the narrator; humor and the repetition of the fun-to-say phrase "It's a … it's a …it's a mitzvah!" that encourages children to chime in as the words are repeated throughout the book. Side notes on each spread explain the specific mitzvah in every vignette. With this aside, parents and teachers have an opportunity to ask the child or group of children, "What is the good deed here?" and spark a conversation without preaching. Children will see how everyday kindness is the beginning of a Jewish journey and a lifetime commitment to *tikkun olam* (repairing the world)—Publisher.

ISBN 978-1-58023-509-9

1. Commandments (Judaism)—Juvenile literature. I. Suneby, Elizabeth, 1958– II. Molk, Laurel. III. Title. IV. Title: It is a mitzvah. V. Title: It is a— it is a— it is a mitzvah.
BM520.7.H395 2012
296.1'8—dc23
2012003703

10 9 8 7 6 5 4 3 2 1

Manufactured in China
Jacket and interior design: Tim Holtz

Published by Jewish Lights Publishing
A Division of Longhill Partners, Inc.
Sunset Farm Offices, Route 4, P.O. Box 237
Woodstock, VT 05091
Tel: (802) 457-4000   Fax: (802) 457-4004
www.jewishlights.com

Award-Winning Children's Books from Jewish Lights

Adam & Eve's First Sunset
God's New Day
by Sandy Eisenberg Sasso
Illustrations by Joani Keller Rothenberg
Explores fear and hope, faith and gratitude, in a way that kids will understand.
For ages 4 & up. 9 x 12, 32 pp, Full-color illus., HC, 978-1-58023-177-0

Also available—a board book for kids 0–4:
Adam & Eve's New Day 978-1-59473-205-8
(SkyLight Paths)

Around the World in One Shabbat
Jewish People Celebrate the Sabbath Together
by Durga Yael Bernhard
Take your child on a colorful adventure to share the many ways Jewish people celebrate Shabbat around the world. *Shabbat Shalom!*
For ages 3–6. 11 x 8½, 32 pp, Full-color illus., HC, 978-1-58023-433-7

Because Nothing Looks Like God
by Lawrence Kushner and Karen Kushner
Illustrations by Dawn W. Majewski
Shows how God is with us every day, in every way.
For ages 4 & up. 11 x 8½, 32 pp, Full-color illus., HC, 978-1-58023-092-6
Also Available: Teacher's Guide by Karen Kushner:
For ages 5–8. 8½ x 11, 22 pp, PB, 978-1-58023-140-4

But God Remembered
Stories of Women from Creation to the Promised Land
by Sandy Eisenberg Sasso
Illustrations by Bethanne Andersen
Four different stories of women briefly mentioned in biblical tradition and religious texts, but never explored.
For ages 8 & up. 9 x 12, 32 pp, Full-color illus., Quality PB, 978-1-58023-372-9

Cain & Abel
Finding the Fruits of Peace
by Sandy Eisenberg Sasso
Illustrations by Joani Keller Rothenberg
A beautiful recasting of the biblical tale. A spiritual conversation-starter about anger and how to deal with it, for parents and children to share.
Ages 5 & up. 9 x 12, 32 pp, Full-color illus., HC, 978-1-58023-123-7

The 11th Commandment
Wisdom from Our Children
by The Children of America
"If there were an Eleventh Commandment, what would it be?"
For all ages. 8 x 10, 48 pp, Full-color illus., HC, 978-1-879045-46-0

For Heaven's Sake
by Sandy Eisenberg Sasso
Illustrations by Kathryn Kunz Finney
Isaiah, a young boy, searches for heaven and learns that it is often found in the places where you least expect it.
For ages 4 & up. 9 x 12, 32 pp, Full-color illus., HC, 978-1-58023-054-4

God in Between
by Sandy Eisenberg Sasso
Illustrations by Sally Sweetland
If you wanted to find God, where would you look? Teaches that God can be found where we are.
For ages 4 & up. 9 x 12, 32 pp, Full-color illus., HC, 978-1-879045-86-6

God's Paintbrush
Special 10th Anniversary Edition
by Sandy Eisenberg Sasso
Illustrations by Annette Compton
Invites children of all faiths and backgrounds to encounter God openly through moments in their own lives—and help the adults who love them to be a part of that encounter.
For ages 4 & up. 11 x 8½, 32 pp, Full-color illus., HC, 978-1-58023-195-4

Also available—a board book version for kids 0–4:
I Am God's Paintbrush 978-1-59473-265-2
(SkyLight Paths)

God's Paintbrush Celebration Kit
A Spiritual Activity Kit for Teachers and Students of All Faiths, All Backgrounds
by Sandy Eisenberg Sasso & Rev. Donald Schmidt
Illustrations by Annette Compton
This indispensable, completely nonsectarian teaching tool is designed for all religious education settings.
Five sessions for eight children ages 5–8.
9 x 12, 40 Full-color activity sheets and teacher folder, 978-1-58023-050-6